Dear Parent:

Congratulations! Your child is taking the first steps on an exciting journey. The destination? Independent reading!

STEP INTO READING® will help your child get there. The program offers five steps to reading success. Each step includes fun stories and colorful art. There are also Step into Reading Sticker Books, Step into Reading Math Readers, Step into Reading Phonics Readers, Step into Reading Write-In Readers, and Step into Reading Phonics Boxed Sets—a complete literacy program with something to interest every child.

Learning to Read, Step by Step!

Ready to Read   Preschool–Kindergarten
• big type and easy words • rhyme and rhythm • picture clues
For children who know the alphabet and are eager to begin reading.

Reading with Help   Preschool–Grade 1
• basic vocabulary • short sentences • simple stories
For children who recognize familiar words and sound out new words with help.

Reading on Your Own   Grades 1–3
• engaging characters • easy-to-follow plots • popular topics
For children who are ready to read on their own.

Reading Paragraphs   Grades 2–3
• challenging vocabulary • short paragraphs • exciting stories
For newly independent readers who read simple sentences with confidence.

Ready for Chapters   Grades 2–4
• chapters • longer paragraphs • full-color art
For children who want to take the plunge into chapter books but still like colorful pictures.

STEP INTO READING® is designed to give every child a successful reading experience. The grade levels are only guides. Children can progress through the steps at their own speed, developing confidence in their reading, no matter what their grade.

Remember, a lifetime love of reading starts with a single step!

For Brianna Twofoot —C.W.

Visit us on the Web!
StepIntoReading.com
randomhouse.com/kids
www.barbie.com

Educators and librarians, for a variety of teaching tools, visit us at randomhouse.com/teachers

ISBN 978-0-307-93122-1 (trade) — ISBN 978-0-375-97081-8 (lib. bdg.)

Printed in the United States of America   10 9 8 7 6 5 4 3 2 1

i can be...
Barbie™
President

By Christy Webster

Illustrated by Kellee Riley

Random House 🏠 New York

Barbie wants to be
class president.
A president
is a leader.

Barbie wants
to make her school
the best.

Raquelle wants
to be president,
too.

Each student can vote
for Barbie or Raquelle.
The girl
with more votes
will get the job.

Barbie gives a speech.
She tells everyone
what she wants to do
as president.

She wants
healthier lunches.
Raquelle wants
more dances.

Barbie's friends help.

They make signs.

They hang

the signs up.

A reporter
from the school paper
asks Barbie
questions.

Barbie meets
many students.
She talks to them
about healthy lunches.

She gives them buttons.
She hopes
they will vote
for her.

Today is election day!

The students vote.

Teresa takes a ballot.

She goes into a booth.

Teresa reads
the ballot.
Who will do
the better job?

She makes a mark.

One vote for Barbie!

The students put
their ballots
in the box.

Teachers count the votes.

Barbie waits
for the results.
Her friends
wait with her.

Barbie has
more votes!
She wins!

Barbie will be
class president!
Her friends
throw a party.

Barbie shakes hands
with Raquelle.
It was a good race.

Barbie asks Raquelle
to be vice president.
Raquelle says yes.
They will be
a great team!

After election day,
a special visitor comes
to Barbie's school.
It is the president
of the United States!

Barbie shows
the president
around her school.

Barbie asks
what it is like
to be the president.

The president lives
in the White House.

She makes laws.

She meets other leaders.

She leads the country.

The president loves
to help people.
Barbie likes
to help people,
too.

The president thinks
Barbie will be
a good leader.

Someday,
Barbie could
be president
of the United States!

For now,
Barbie will work hard
for her school.

Two presidents
go on the stage.
Barbie can be

a great president!